LITTLE LAMB

For Regan

First published in 2003 by Macmillan Children's Books
a division of Macmillan Publishers Limited
20 New Wharf Road
London N1 9RR
Basingstoke and Oxford
Associated companies worldwide
www.panmacmillan.com

Produced by Fernleigh Books
1A London Road, Enfield
Middlesex EN2 6BN

Text copyright © 2003 by Fernleigh Books
Illustrations copyright © 2003 by Piers Harper

ISBN 1-405-02060-1 (HB)
ISBN 1-405-02061-X (PB)

1 3 5 7 9 8 6 4 2 (HB)
1 3 5 7 9 8 6 4 2 (PB)

A CIP catalogue record for this book is available
from the British Library.

Printed in China

LITTLE LAMB

Illustrated by Piers Harper

Little Lamb and Mama Sheep lived in a green, green field with lots of other mama sheep and their babies.

The lambs' favourite game was hide-and-seek.
"Come and find me!" bleated Little Lamb
to the others, and she skipped
away to find a place to hide.

Little Lamb headed for a leafy bush
at the edge of the field.
  "They won't find me behind here!"
she giggled to herself. But behind the
bush, she saw that there was another green,
green field beyond.

  And in that green, green field was
an animal she had never seen before . . .

"Baa!" said Little Lamb. "I'm Little Lamb and I'm looking for a good place to hide. Can you help me?"

"MOO!" said the cow. "You don't want to hide in this field, Little Lamb. You might get trampled on. Why don't you go over to the sty? That's a good place to hide for a little thing like you."

So Little Lamb skipped over to the sty.

"Baa!" said the Little Lamb. "I'm Little Lamb
and I'm looking for a good place to hide.
Can you help me?"

"Oink, oink!" said the pigs. "You don't want to hide in our pigsty, Little Lamb. You'll get your lovely white fleece all muddy. Why don't you go down to the pond? That's a good place to hide for a clean thing like you."

So Little Lamb skipped down to the pond.

"Baa!" said Little Lamb. "I'm Little Lamb
and I'm looking for a good place to hide.
Can you help me?"

"Quack, quack!" said the duck. "You don't
want to hide near this pond, Little Lamb.
You might fall in. Go back to your mama.
That's the best place for a young
thing like you."

Little Lamb wandered off to look for her mama.
  "Where is she hiding?" said Little Lamb,
but there was no one to hear her.
  "I don't know where my mama is!"
And Little Lamb started to cry.

"Found you!" said a friendly voice. Looking up, Little Lamb
saw a pair of big, brown, familiar eyes. It was Piper, the sheepdog.
  "Well, Little Lamb, what a good hiding place!
But you shouldn't have gone so far away.
Your friends have been looking
everywhere for you, and your
mama is worried.
Let's go home."

So Little Lamb followed Piper across the farmyard
and up into the sheep's green, green field. And there was Mama
Sheep, smiling and bleating, happy that Little Lamb was home.
  "Baa! Baa!" said Little Lamb, rushing to Mama Sheep's side.
"Baa!" said all the sheep.

"Thank you, Piper," called Mama Sheep.

"Just doing my job!" said Piper, and he raced back towards the farm.

Little Lamb nuzzled her mother. The next time she played hide-and-seek, she thought, she wouldn't stray from the green, green field, or too far from her mama's warm and cosy side.